A portion of the money you pay for this book goes to Children's Television Workshop.
It is put right back into "Sesame Street" and other CTW educational projects.
Thanks for helping!

http://www.randomhouse.com/
http://www.sesamestreet.com

Library of Congress Cataloging-in-Publication Data
St. Pierre, Stephanie.
It's not easy being big! / by Stephanie St. Pierre ; illustrated by John Lund.
    p.   cm. — (A bright & early book)   SUMMARY: Big Bird discovers that some things
are easy to do if you are small and others are easy to do if you are big.
ISBN 0-679-88810-1 (trade) — ISBN 0-679-98810-6 (lib. bdg.)
[1. Size—Fiction. 2. Birds—Fiction. 3. Puppets—Fiction.]
I. Lund, John (John H.), ill. II. Title. III. Series:
PZ7.S14355It 1998 [E]—dc21 97-18050

Printed in the United States of America   10 9 8 7 6 5 4 3 2

It's Not Easy Being Big!

By Stephanie
St. Pierre

Illustrated by
John Lund

A Bright & Early Book
From Beginner Books
A Division of Random House, Inc.

Random House/Children's Television Workshop

Sometimes
it's not easy
being big.

Too big to swing.

Too big to ride.

Too big to play.

Too big to hide.

It's not easy
being big.

Big Bird seesaws down.

Elmo seesaws up.

It's
not easy
being
small.

Too small to see.

Too small to cross.

Too small to reach.

Too small to toss.

It's not easy
being small.

Small.

Smaller.   Smallest.

Teeny-tiny Twiddlebugs!

Big.   Bigger.

Biggest.

Super-duper Snuffle-upagus!

Big ball.

Small ball.

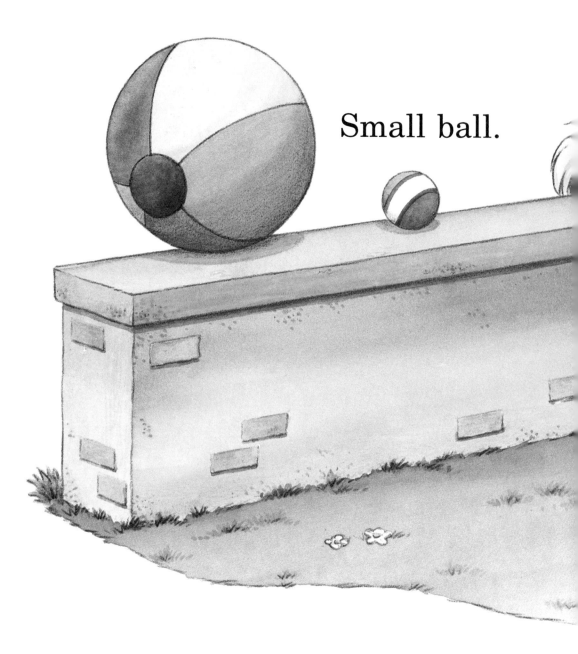

Balls on the wall.

Big, bigger, biggest.

Small, smaller, smallest.

Balls on the wall!

Big, bigger, biggest.
Small, smaller, smallest.
Balls off the wall!

Time to play ball!

High ball.

Low ball.

Balls
over,
under,
around,
and
through!

Big Bird is big.

Elmo is small.

Sometimes it's easy being big. Sometimes it's easy being small.

That's all.